IZZY the INVENTOR

and the TEENY-TINY Ogres

USBORNE QUICKLINKS

DISCOVER EXPERIMENTS LIKE THE ONES IZZY TRIES IN THIS BOOK
AND FIND OUT MORE ABOUT THE SCIENCE BEHIND THEM...

AT USBORNE QUICKLINKS WE HAVE PROVIDED LINKS
TO WEBSITES WHERE YOU CAN:

• Catch iron in your food with a magnet experiment.

• Watch a video about collecting insects with a pooter.

• Experiment with forces and make a balloon rocket.

• Find lots more experiments to try at home.

TO VISIT THESE SITES, GO TO USBORNE.COM/QUICKLINKS
AND TYPE IN THE KEYWORDS "IZZY AND THE OGRES" OR
SCAN THE QR CODE ON THIS PAGE.

PLEASE FOLLOW THE INTERNET SAFETY GUIDELINES
AT USBORNE QUICKLINKS.

CHILDREN SHOULD BE SUPERVISED ONLINE.

Izzy the INVENTOR

and the TEENY-TINY Ogres

Zanna Davidson

ILLUSTRATED by Elissa Elwick

Contents

Meet Izzy 6

CHAPTER ONE
A Teeny-Tiny Mistake 8

CHAPTER TWO
Inventions and
Disguises 20

CHAPTER THREE
Iron Teeth 36

CHAPTER FOUR
Total Chaos
52

CHAPTER FIVE
Science is for
Everyone
74

CHAPTER SIX
The Tickle Machine
94

Science Experiments
122

Meet Izzy

She wants to be the...

Greatest Inventor

of **ALL** time.

Izzy always believed in **SCIENCE**, *not* magic. But then, one day, something unexpected happened. A fairy appeared in her bedroom, saying...

It is I, Rose Petal Twinkle-Toes, your Fairy Godmother.

The fairy gave Izzy a unicorn (which she hadn't asked for)...

...and sent her on a mission to Fairytale Land (which she didn't believe in).

From that moment on, life for Izzy would never be the same again...

CHAPTER ONE
A teeny-tiny Mistake

Izzy had made a mistake. A **teeny-tiny** one. She'd gone to 𝒯airytale 𝒧and to rescue her best friend, Henry the unicorn, from being squished by MASSIVE ogres...

She'd managed to *shrink* the ogres...

...and **save** Henry.

Hooray!

But somehow she'd brought the ogres back with her and last night they had...

...ESCAPED!

Now Izzy had **TWO** fairies in her bedroom, telling her off – Rose Petal Twinkle-Toes, and Brenda.

We need those ogres back!

Things in Fairytale Land are going VERY wrong without them.

Brenda used to be a **bad** fairy, but she was now *trying* to be good. Although, looking at her terrifying expression, Izzy wasn't sure it was working.

"We've brought Henry to help you," said Fairy Rose Petal. "Together, you must **FIND THE OGRES** and bring them back to 𝓕airytale 𝓛and."

"I'm sorry," said Izzy. "But I don't understand... isn't it **good** that the ogres have gone?"

No, it isn't! You've upset the delicate balance of our world, Izzy.

Normally, the ogres keep the wolves and bears under control...

But now, the wolves and bears are chasing the witches and wizards!

So the witches and wizards aren't keeping an eye on the goblins...

Our wands!

...who are tormenting the fairies.

And without the fairies, NOTHING in Fairytale Land gets done!

Where is my fairy godmother?

"Oh, I *see*!" said Izzy. She quickly started to draw. "It's like a food pyramid with the top predator missing!"

I don't like seeing fairies at the bottom.

"We've no time for this chit-chat," said Still-Quite-Scary-Brenda. "Just find those ogres. Or **ELSE**."

"Or **ELSE** *what*?" asked Izzy.

"Or you'll **NEVER** be welcome in 𝓕airytale 𝓛and again!" snapped Fairy Brenda. "And that includes you, too, Henry."

Brenda — you're still sounding a lot like a BAD FAIRY.

I'm learning to be good. It takes time.

"The thing is," said Izzy, "there's an **INVENTION COMPETITION** today at the TOWN HALL. I *really* want to enter, but I haven't tested my invention yet."

I need time to work on it!

Fairy Brenda **shrugged**. "Not our problem," she said, and held out a tiny silver bell.

Ring this once you've found the ogres.

CHAPTER TWO
Inventions and Disguises

Izzy gave Henry a hug and a cookie. "Don't worry," she said. "We'll find those ogres!"

The Mystery of the Missing Ogres

What do we know about the ogres?

* They make LOUD grunting noises.

* They are mostly made of stone.

* In Fairytale Land they are famous for being MEAN and TERRIFYING.

* They like going on RAMPAGES.

* They are now about 6cm high (since we shrank them with water balloons on our last trip to FAIRYTALE LAND).

* There are NINE of them.

Where should we look for them?

* The ogres were last seen
  at 9pm last night,
  heading over the rooftops.

* The ogres then disappeared into **THE PARK**.

Who is on the case?

* Izzy the Inventor

* Henry the **Amazing** Unicorn!

* Bella (my little sister) was also at the scene
of the ogres' disappearance.
Unfortunately, she can't help
now as she's gone to
her kung-fu class.

"First stop, the park! It doesn't take long to get there," Izzy went on, showing Henry her map.

"But how are we going to CATCH the ogres?" asked Henry.

"Luckily," said Izzy, "I have some **catching** and **trapping** inventions! They were made for creepy-crawlies but they should work just as well on tiny ogres..."

A telescope for *spotting* them!

A friendly bug catcher might trap them...

"And I have a little magic bag to put them in," said Henry. "What's more, if we find the ogres quickly, you can still go to your **COMPETITION**. And I can help you! Er, what is your invention?"

"It's meant to be a tickle machine," said Izzy. "But, so far, all I've done is draw a plan..."

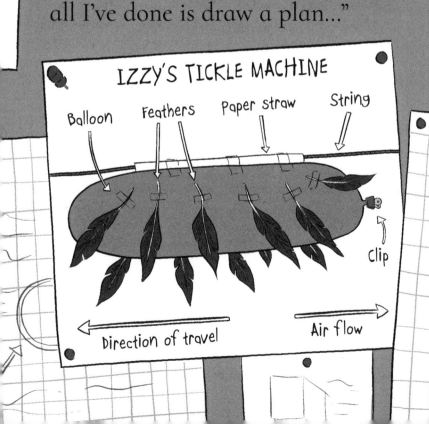

IZZY'S TICKLE MACHINE

Balloon Feathers Paper straw String

Clip

← Direction of travel

Air flow →

"I came up with the idea because I'm **really** ticklish," said Izzy. "But I'm not sure it will work."

The air flowing out of the balloon should push it along the string in the opposite direction.

But what if the straw gets stuck? Or the air comes out too fast?

"Mmm," said Henry. He was trying to look as if he was listening to everything Izzy was saying. But really he was thinking about **cake**.

"Never mind," said Izzy, laughing. "I'll work it out." And she started packing her SCIENCE bag.

I'll take my science notebook...

My map of Fairytale Land – just in case...

My CATCHING and TRAPPING inventions...

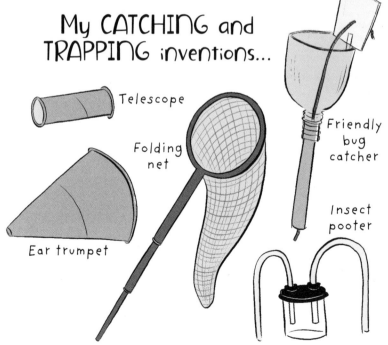

Telescope

Folding net

Friendly bug catcher

Ear trumpet

Insect pooter

Other useful things...

 Wire

 Magnets

 Sticky tape

 Screwdriver

 Compass

Scissors

 Magnifying glass

And everything I need for my tickle machine!

Hopefully, I'll get the chance to work on it.

"Sorry," said Henry, as Izzy packed. "I'm not much help, am I? I could never come up with inventions like you do."

29

That's not true. Science is for EVERYONE!

"Do you really think I could invent something too?" asked Henry.

"Of course you could," said Izzy. "I believe in you!"

"In that case," said Henry, "I will think about new inventions. Maybe something to do with cookies..."

And now, just as excitingly, we're going on an ADVENTURE. To a park!

I've never been to a park before.

"Um..." said Izzy. "I'm not sure it's a good idea for you to come **with me** to the park, Henry..."

"**WHY NOT?**" asked Henry.

"Even though *I* believe in you, most people in my world... *don't*. The closest thing we have to unicorns are horses."

"Well, in that case," said Henry, "I will come to the park **DISGUISED** as a horse!"

Izzy sighed and shook her head. "The only way you could come is if you were **invisible**."

"Wow! You really are invisible!" said Izzy. "Ogre-catching mission here we come!"

CHAPTER THREE
Iron Teeth

Half an hour later, Izzy's dad had brought Izzy to the park. (And Henry, although he didn't know it.)

Everything had gone smoothly
– apart from when Henry had
tripped on the pavement
and said,

"Oh! Galloping goblins!"

very loudly and his
cloak had slipped off.

Izzy's dad had looked confused
for a moment, but Izzy
distracted him by
hopping around as
if she'd just stubbed
her toe.

Now Izzy's dad was reading a book, leaving Izzy and Henry free to search for the **TINY OGRES**.

"How about I try **shaking** the bush – and then you can catch the ogres as they come out!" whispered Henry.

"Excellent," said Izzy.

Unfortunately, the ogres
were too FAST...

The ogres were also VERY SNEAKY.

"Now all the ogres are back in the bush," sighed Izzy. "How will we EVER get them out?" Then she looked down at her net and spotted a large hole. "And how did **that** get there?" she wondered.

"Oops," said Henry. "I forgot to mention... Ogres have

IRON TEETH."

Izzy's eyes lit up.

That's excellent!

It is?

"Iron is magnetic," explained Izzy. "That means they'll be attracted to MAGNETS! All we need to do now is make a MAGNET CATCHER!"

Izzy flicked through her **SCIENCE NOTEBOOK**...

Here we go!

HOW TO MAKE A MAGNET CATCHER
By Izzy

What you need:
- a stick

- sticky tape

- a large magnet

What to do:

1. Tape your magnet to the end of a long stick.

2. Hold your MAGNET CATCHER near to the object you want to attract.

* The object will need to be a magnetic metal, like IRON or STEEL.

3. You don't have to touch the object, as your magnet will pull the object towards it, as long as the object isn't too heavy.

Your MAGNET CATCHER will also work through water...

It will even work through solid objects, like cardboard.

4. You can use your MAGNET CATCHER to find out which metals are attracted to magnets.

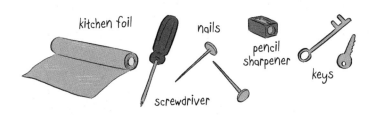

kitchen foil

nails

pencil sharpener

keys

screwdriver

How do magnets work?

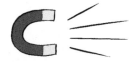

Magnets are metals that attract some other metals, like iron or steel. They do this because they create an invisible force around them, called a MAGNETIC FORCE. The area of this invisible force is known as a MAGNETIC FIELD. If a magnetic object is inside the magnetic field, it gets attracted to the magnet and moves towards it, even without anyone touching it.

Extra note

Not all metals are attracted by magnets. Objects that contain iron or steel are attracted most strongly. Magnets have no effect on kitchen foil, which is made of aluminium.

"We've made a **MAGNET CATCHER!**" said Izzy. "Now, pass me the magic ogre bag please, Henry?" Then she plunged the catcher into the bush...

1... 2... ogres!

3... 4... 5...

"I'll ring my silver bell," said Henry, pulling it from his bag.

DING! DING!

At once, a sparkly pink mist appeared.

We just need to go through the mist and we'll be in Fairytale Land.

But what if my dad notices I've gone?

"We won't be long," said Henry. "And you always say that when you get back from Fairytale Land, it's as if no time has passed at all."

Izzy looked at her dad, but he was deep in his book.

"*Please*, Izzy," begged Henry. "Okay," said Izzy, holding tight to the bag of squirming ogres. "I'll come to *Fairytale Land!*"

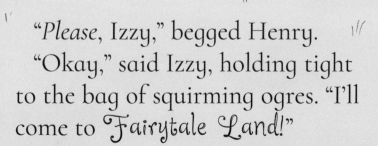

Izzy climbed onto Henry's back...

...and missed.

Oh... warts and wizards!

It's hard getting onto an invisible unicorn.

Izzy tried again...

...and **MADE IT!**

Then they **trotted** through
the shimmery mist into
Fairytale Land.

CHAPTER FOUR
Total Chaos

"Phew!" said Henry, taking off his **invisibility** cloak. "It was really hot under there."

SLEEPING
BEAUTY'S
CASTLE

FROZEN WASTES
(HOME TO THE WICKED
WINTER PIXIES)

IMPENETRABLE THORNY FOREST

YET MORE
FAIRYTALE
WOODS

FOREVER SUMMER
MEADOWS

RUMPELSTILTSKIN'S HOUSE

FAIRYLAND FARM

SNOW WHITE'S
COTTAGE

"I think that's a farm over there," said Izzy, pointing to the left. "So maybe we're near Fairyland Farm."

"I mean... **GET DOWN!**" cried Henry. "There's a flock of fairies flying towards us. **VERY FAST.** We need to take cover."

Henry and Izzy ducked behind a nearby bush, just as a hundred fairies flew past at a hundred miles an hour.

The fairies were followed by a band of goblins, shooting mud pies at them.

After the goblins came
some very worried-looking
witches and wizards.

Then... **nothing**.
"Perhaps it's safe to come out now?" said Izzy.

Rawwwr!

There was the sound of more **thuds**. "Oh no! What's next?" said Henry, covering his eyes. **"Three-headed giants?"**

"It's okay!" said Izzy. "It's the Rhyming Rabbits!"

And they don't look very happy!

"No wonder Fairy Rose Petal and Brenda aren't here to meet us," said Henry. "It's just as Fairy Rose Petal said – everything's **IN CHAOS**."

"Well, we can't hang about here," said Izzy. "We need to find shelter, then work out what to do!" She looked again at the map. "That cottage over there looks safe..."

The Rhyming Rabbits fluttered off. Izzy and Henry could hear yet more **ROARING** noises, getting closer and closer.

Quick, Henry! To Snow White's Cottage. As fast as you can!

Snow White's Cottage seemed very tranquil compared to the rest of Fairytale Land.

"I expect you know all about me already," said Snow White. "I am the fairest of them all."

"Sorry," said Izzy. "I don't think I've read your fairy tale..."

Snow White looked shocked. "But I'm the most FAMOUS fairytale princess. I have all the best qualities..."

"That's wonderful," said Izzy. "But we're in a bit of a rush. Fairytale Land is in chaos and we have to find Fairy Rose Petal and Brenda. Do you know where they might be?"

They're on their way! They told me to expect you...

I thought we could all have some cake.

Did someone say 'cake'?

69

Izzy sat down on a handy tree stump. She wanted a moment of quiet so she could think about her **tickle machine**. But then she heard a croaky voice.

Hello, dearie. Would you like an apple?

A beautiful, red, shiny apple?

Izzy took the apple and raised it to her lips.

At that exact moment, Henry came out of the cottage with the cake.

But Henry was TOO LATE. Izzy took a bite of the apple...

Noooooooooooooooooooooo!

...and fell,
lifeless,
to the
ground.

CHAPTER FIVE

Science is for Everyone

After that, it seemed to Henry as if everything happened **VERY** fast. The wicked stepmother threw off her disguise and ran off, **cackling**. Then the seven dwarfs came home.

"Snow White is fine!" said Henry. "But look what's happened to my friend. She's under a spell!"

The seven dwarfs took one look at Izzy, and popped her into a glass coffin.

"What are you doing?" cried Henry. "We just need to find a way to break the spell."

That's MY coffin!

Please, take Izzy out!

"NO ONE MUST TOUCH HER until the prince comes," said Dwarf Bushy Beard.

"You know the laws of **FAIRYTALE LAND**, Henry," said Dwarf Red Cap, sternly. "Fairy tales are NOT to be messed with."

Henry knew this to be true. In the past, meddling with fairy tales had led to...

...vanishing princes...

...badly-behaved fairies...

...and the tiny, troublesome ogres (which had plunged Fairytale Land into all this chaos).

81

"But Izzy doesn't *belong* in Fairytale Land," said Henry. "She's got an **INVENTION COMPETITION** to go to."

Then he gave a cry of relief as Fairy Rose Petal and Brenda fluttered into view.

Hello, everyone!

"Oh dear," said Fairy Rose Petal, peering into the coffin.

"I'm afraid Izzy will just have to wait for the prince to come along."
"But that could take AGES!" said Henry.

What's more, I don't think Izzy WANTS to marry a prince.

Her dream is to be the greatest inventor in the world.

"Well, she should have read her fairy tales," said Fairy Brenda. "Then she'd know better than to take shiny red apples from strangers."

This ISN'T FAIR!

"I'd love to stay and help," said Fairy Rose Petal, "but we must sort out these ogres. They're no good to us tiny."

"We need to work out how to get them back to their normal size so they can restore order to *Fairytale Land*," added Fairy Brenda.

"Oh dear, what a **PICKLE**," said Dwarf Long Nose.

"Can't you cast a **magic spell** with your horn, Henry?" asked Snow White.

No. The only magic I can do is glitter. And rainbows.

"But that's not going to wake up Izzy, is it?" said Henry. "What are we going to do? Izzy's my **BEST FRIEND** in the **WORLD**."

"We're going to have to work this out for ourselves," said Henry. "Let me think... what would Izzy do?"

Henry thought for a long time.

How do I know what Izzy would do? I'm not Izzy. This is HARD.

Ooh. I haven't had any of the cake yet.

Stop thinking about cake, Henry. You have to save your friend.

I think it's a chocolate cake. I hope it's moist.

"SCIENCE will solve the problem!" Henry announced, through a mouthful of cake.

And here is Izzy's science bag!

"But we don't KNOW any science..." said Dwarf Knobbly Knees, doubtfully.

"I should think not," snapped Snow White. "Science isn't for the likes of you. And it's *certainly* **NOT** for me."

"Actually," said Henry,
"Science is for
EVERYONE!
And that includes princesses
AND dwarfs."

With those words, Henry took
a deep breath and opened Izzy's
science notebook.

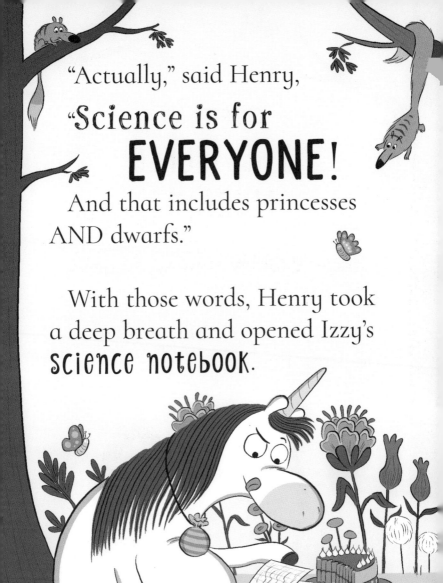

CHAPTER SIX
The Tickle Machine

"I know **exactly** how we're going to break the spell on Izzy," said Henry, proudly. "And *without* touching her."

"How?" demanded Snow White.
"We're going to make a **TICKLE MACHINE!**" said Henry.

I remember Izzy saying that she is VERY ticklish.

And if we make a tickle machine, then we can wake Izzy WITHOUT touching her.

"But I wouldn't even know where to begin," said Snow White.

"It's okay," said Henry. "We have Izzy's instructions..."

THE TICKLE MACHINE
by Izzy

What you need:

- string
- a straw
- sticky tape
- a balloon

- a bulldog clip
- feathers
- scissors
- 2 volunteers

1. Cut a piece of string, about 3m (10ft) long, and thread it through a straw.

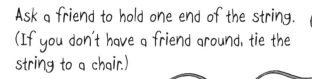

Ask a friend to hold one end of the string. (If you don't have a friend around, tie the string to a chair.)

2. Blow up a balloon. Hold the neck closed with a bulldog clip.

3. Tape the balloon to the straw, like this.

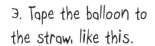

4. Tape feathers to the underside of the balloon, like this.

5. Push the balloon to one end of the string, with the neck of the balloon facing you, and pull the string tight.

6. Ask a volunteer to stand or sit under the middle of the string.

7. Take the bulldog clip off the balloon.

As the air comes out of the balloon, it is pushed along the string, tickling as it goes.

"For this to work, I think we need two dwarfs, to stand at either end of the coffin," said Henry. Dwarf Long Nose and Bushy Beard hurried into position.

"I've cut the string with my teeth," said Henry. "Snow White, can you thread it through the straw?"

"Really?" asked Snow White. "Do I have to?"

"I'm afraid my hooves aren't very good at delicate operations," sniffed Henry.

I'll pretend it's sewing!

101

When everything was in place,
they all crowded around the coffin.
"I do hope this works," said Henry.
"Here goes..." said Snow White,
unclipping the balloon.

The balloon
WHOOSHED
forward...

...the feathers
brushed over
Izzy's face.

She sneezed...

...and spluttered...

...then sat up
and laughed.

We've broken the spell!

Hooray for science!

"What's going on?" asked Izzy, looking very confused.

Before anyone could explain, there came the sound of hoofbeats.

TRIT! TROT! TRIT! TROT!

"**QUICK**, Izzy! Out!" cried Snow White, waving her away.

Izzy climbed out of the glass coffin and Snow White **leaped** inside, lay down, closed her eyes... and smiled.

Ooh! Quick work!

Moments later, a dashing prince rode up.

Henry couldn't resist joining in.

This beautiful princess has eaten a poisoned apple!

The prince gazed down at Snow White.

Oh but I love her!

Have you even MET? This is all happening a bit fast.

Snow White quickly opened her eyes, before Izzy could say anything else.

"My prince!" she cried. "Your love has saved me. Let us ride away together and live happily ever after."

The prince lifted Snow White onto his horse. Snow White winked at Izzy and whispered to her...

Thank you! Also — great notebook.

"So many wonderful ideas in it," Snow White went on. "I'm taking it with me – I hope you don't mind. I thought it might come in handy."

"You **CAN'T** take my science notebook!" Izzy called out.

But it was TOO LATE. Snow White and the prince were already galloping away.

"Oh, that's lucky," said Fairy Rose Petal, fluttering into view. "You've managed to wake Izzy. Well done, everyone."

And we bring good news...

"The ogres are back to their enormous size," said Fairy Brenda, "and are rampaging across Fairytale Land again."

"So you're free to go home again, Izzy," said Fairy Rose Petal. "And go to your **INVENTION COMPETITION**."

"I haven't had time to practise. Even worse, Snow White has gone off with my **SCIENCE NOTEBOOK!**" wailed Izzy.

You ate a poisoned apple and fell into a DEEP and MAGICAL sleep.

But Snow White, the dwarfs and I made your tickle machine.

It was your TICKLE MACHINE that broke the spell.

Now I'm a scientist too!

Izzy made it to the **INVENTION COMPETITION** just in time. The tickle machine worked perfectly.

But the best part, Izzy thought, was knowing that Henry was there too, sitting in the audience, **Cheering** her on. Even if he was invisible.

Afterwards, Izzy gave Henry a huge hug. "Thank you for helping me," she said.

"And without *you*," said Henry, "I would never have known that **science** is for

everyone.

Even **unicorns**."

"**ESPECIALLY** unicorns," smiled Izzy. Then Henry rang the silver bell until the sparkly mist appeared.

Goodbye, Izzy. See you soon!

That night, before bed, Izzy decided to check her book of fairy tales. She was curious to know what had become of Snow White...

Snow White

After the Prince and Snow White rode away to the Prince's castle, Snow White sat down and read the science notebook that was to change her life.

"Science is AMAZING!" announced Snow White.

She showed the notebook to the Prince, who was just as enthusiastic. They turned the entire left wing of the castle into a GIANT laboratory.

Soon, Snow White was SO GOOD at science that her wicked stepmother never dared go near her again.

Snow White

The Seven Dwarfs came to live with Snow White and worked as her laboratory assistants. "We have new names," they decided. "From now on, we only answer to Magnetism, Electricity, Spark, Bunsen, Burner, Experiment and Bob."

They were often visited by the most famous scientist of all, Henry the Unicorn, inventor of the COOKIE MACHINE.

The End

That is the best fairy tale ending EVER!

Make an insect pooter
- with a bit of grown-up help

What you need:

- Glass jar with a screw lid
- Strong sticky tape
- 2 Bendy straws
- Large nail
- Sturdy hammer
- Scissors
- Small piece of muslin or old tights

1. Using the nail and the hammer, make 2 small holes in the lid of the jar, about 1.5cm-2.5cm apart.

2. Turn over the lid and bang the hammer on the holes, to smooth down the edges.

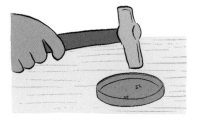

*if you don't have a glass jar you can use a plastic container with a lid. Use the end of a compass, or a pair of sharp nail scissors, to make the holes, then widen them by pushing a pencil into the hole. You can make the holes either in the lid or on either side of the plastic container.

3. Cut the ends off the straws. The bottom of the straws should come about halfway down the jar (see bottom pic).

4. Push the straws through the holes and hold them in place with tape or sticky putty.

5. Wind the muslin over and around the end of one of the straws. Secure it with sticky tape. Mark this straw with a pen. This is your mouth straw!

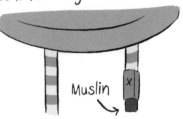

Muslin

6. Screw the lid on the jar. To catch a bug, place the unmarked straw near an insect and then suck on the mouth straw.

Always suck through the mouth straw — the muslin will stop insects going into your mouth!

Only try catching bugs that are smaller than the end of the straw and avoid dangerous bugs, like wasps or bees.

Make a friendly bug catcher
– with a bit of grown-up help

What you need:

- 1.25l plastic drinks bottle (with straight sides)
- Piece of thin, strong card • String • Craft knife
- 1 Washer • 1 Screw • Long cardboard tube, about 2.5cm wide (e.g. an old wrapping-paper tube) • Strong sticky tape
- Small piece of paper about 10cm x 8cm

1. Draw a line halfway down the bottle. Then ask a grown-up to cut along the line using a craft knife.

2. Fold the wider end of the bottle width-wise and pinch the top of each side. Then fold in the other direction and pinch the top again, so you have four corners.

3. Press down firmly about 4cm from each corner to shape the sides.

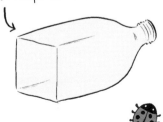

4. To make the lid, cut the card about 1cm wider than the bottle on three sides (see step 5). Punch a hole in the centre with scissors.

5. Attach the lid to one side of the bottle with sticky tape.

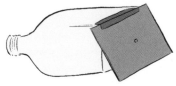

6. Attach the tube to the other end of the bottle with tape.

7. Place the string in the middle of the paper and roll the paper into a tight cone shape around it. Secure the cone shape with tape. Tie one end of the string to the screw.

8. Thread the other end of the string through the hole in the cardboard lid and tie a knot to secure it.

9. Drop the string through the bottle and tube, so it comes out the other end. Place the cone in the opening, where the tube meets the bottle, and tape it in place. The cone stops bugs falling out of the other end of the tube.

Only try catching bugs that are bigger than the hole in the cardboard tube!

Lastly, replace the screw with a washer.

How does the tickle machine work?

To understand the TICKLE MACHINE,
you need to know about
FORCES.

→ A FORCE is a push or a pull that makes an
object do something. Without forces, nothing
would ever start moving!

The TICKLE MACHINE uses a PUSHING force.

As the balloon deflates, it pushes the air out of the
neck of the balloon. The air flowing out pushes the
balloon along the string in the OPPOSITE direction.

Another example would be if you threw a ball
while wearing roller skates! The force of you

throwing the ball would
push the ball forward.
But in reaction, another
force would push you
backwards, in the exact
opposite direction.

This is from a famous scientific rule:

Every action has an equal and opposite reaction.

Isaac Newton

SCIENCE SAFETY

ALWAYS TAKE EXTRA CARE WITH HOT OR SHARP THINGS
AND NEVER PUT ANYTHING IN YOUR MOUTH. IF AN
ACTIVITY INVOLVES DOING SOMETHING YOU MIGHT NOT
USUALLY DO, ASK YOUR GROWN-UP TO HELP YOU.

Series designer: Brenda Cole
Series editor: Lesley Sims
Cover design by Katie Miller
and Hannah Cobley